GOWNS

Robert Chantler

Typeset in Arial 12pt

Published by
THE FREE THEATRE COMPANY PRESS
Shepperton, Middlesex TW17 8HG

ISBN – 978 0-9561352-6-1

CHARACTERS

JACQUI HILLMAN – beautiful, flirtatious undergraduate

TRISTAN CAMPBELL – handsome medical student, rugby
player

ANDREW CALLAN – B.A. student, Jacqui's first love,
American

WILLIAM HUNTER BLETCHINGLEY – elderly professor

HELEN HUNTER BLETCHINGLEY – his timid, mousy wife

MR and MRS HILLMAN

MR and MRS CALLAN

MR and MRS CAMPBELL

PAUL – Tristan's bi-sexual friend

AISHA – Andrew's fiancée, lives in L.A.

PORTER

AMBULANCE MAN

VICAR

TAXI DRIVER

VICE CHANCELLOR

PRAELECTOR

STEPHANIE ANNE RICE (NO LINES)

PROLOGUE: LOC. KINGS CROSS STATION

MRS HILLMAN:

(snivels) Oh, my little girl.

JACQUI:

I'll be fine mum. You're coming up to see me aren't you?

MRS HILLMAN:

Whenever you want.

MR HILLMAN:

And you can come home and see us whenever you want.

JACQUI:

I love you!

MRS HILLMAN:

I love you too darling.

MR HILLMAN:

We're so proud of you darling. The first in our family ever to go to Cambridge.

JACQUI:

I *am* excited. It's just…I'll miss you, that's all.

MRS HILLMAN:

We'll miss you too darling.

MR HILLMAN:

You find a nice young man.

JACQUI:

You know me.

Scene 1: INT: FORMAL HALLS IN DINING ROOM: AGNES COLLEGE: NIGHT

(The students are at table and there is a general murmur...)

JACQUI:

(sees free seat and approaches. ANDREW is sitting next to it.)

Um, excuse me.

ANDREW:

(looks up and smiles)

Yes?

JACQUI:

Do you mind if I join you?

ANDREW:

Delighted.

JACQUI:

(slight smile) Thanks. (pause) I'm Jacqui Hillman by the way, and I'm studying psychology.

ANDREW:

I'm Andrew Callan. I'm doing a PhD here. I did a B.A. at Kings but I have more friends here so I thought I'd do my doctorate here, and now I have one more friend.

JACQUI:

Why don't you come to my room one evening?

ANDREW:

You don't waste any time, do you? (pause) I'd love to.

JACQUI:

That's a date then. First arch, first floor, first courtyard. A6.

ANDREW:

Thanks.

(The gong is sounded and all stand as the dignitaries file in)

(Fade to...)

Scene 2: INT: JACQUI'S ROOM: NIGHT

(The fire is on and JACQUI is undressing for bed)

JACQUI:

(looks thoughtful, heard in voice over) I hope we can be
more than just friends, Andrew.

(glances at papers on bed) I wonder what my supervisor will
be like. (gets into bed) Oh well, I'll find out tomorrow.

(lights go out)

Scene 3: LOC: BARRINGTON: DAY

(The bus stops at the quiet country stop. JACQUI alights and
walks a little way to a quaint cottage. She knocks on the
door. She hears shuffling from inside, then the door opens.)

WILLIAM:

Oh my dear, you must be Jacqui. (takes hand and kisses it)
Come in, come in.

(door closes)

SCENE 4: INT: WILLIAM'S LOUNGE: DAY

WILLIAM:

(enters first with JACQUI behind)

Come through and take a seat, Jacqui?

JACQUI:

Thank you.

WILLIAM:

Tea?

JACQUI:

Please, Professor.

WILLIAM:

William, please. I'm sure my wife will oblige us. (calls)

Helen!

HELEN:

(enters) Yes dear. (to Jacqui) Hello dear.

JACQUI:

Hello, Mrs Hunter Bletchingley

WILLIAM:

Call her Helen, she won't mind. Will you dear?

HELEN:

Er, no.

WILLIAM:

This is Jacqui. She's one of my new students. Would you do some teas dear?

HELEN:

Of course.

(she leaves)

WILLIAM:

So, Jacqui, do you like the place?

JACQUI:

Very quaint.   Love the garden.

WILLIAM:

Ah yes. Helen does keep it beautifully doesn't she. All our visitors say how lovely it is. It's her greatest love, even more than s... anything else.

HELEN:

(re-enters with tea tray)

Here we are.

WILLIAM and JACQUI:

Thanks.

WILLIAM:

Will you join us dear?

HELEN:

Oh no. I don't want to disturb your discussion. I'll have mine in the kitchen.

(exits)

WILLIAM:

(sips his tea and stares wistfully at Jacqui)

JACQUI:

(awkwardly) Are you alright, William?

WILLIAM:

Wh... oh, yes. Forgive me. You remind me so much of my daughter, that's all. (passes photograph) Judy. She works in the city, in stocks and shares. She visits occasionally but they do such long hours.

JACQUI:

So, what am I in store for this year then?

WILLIAM:

Well, you won't be short of suitors. Randy lot the students are here. The ones that aren't homosexual of course. (chuckles quietly)

JACQUI:

(blank look) Hmmm.

WILLIAM:

You'll certainly enjoy the course. It's one of the best. I got my B.A. in Psychology here in 1950. Went to the other place to do my PhD.

JACQUI:

You went to Oxford then?

WILLIAM:

Oh yes, but I always cheer for Cambridge to win the Boat Race, so that's alright. When I was young, I was a strapping lad. I made the eight, that's the rowing team you know. I was coxen one year. The reason for our little chat is just so we get to know each other, and as I am responsible for your welfare as well as your studies, you can always come to me if you have any problems, worries etc. Any time, I'm usually here. I don't get out much these days.

JACQUI:
Thank you, I will.

(Fade)

Later...

WILLIAM:
It's been nice meeting you, Jacqui. Take care now.

HELEN:
(calls) William!

WILLIAM:
Oh, I think I'm wanted.

JACQUI:
See you soon. Bye.

(She walks away up the path, and WILLIAM just watches)

(Fade)

Scene 5: INT: ANDREW'S LOUNGE: NIGHT

(The room is modestly furnished and very peaceful)

ANDREW:

I have a few close friends here. Paul's my closest friend.
He's bisexual.

JACQUI:

Uh huh.

ANDREW:

He wouldn't mind me teling you that, of course.

JACQUI:

Why don't you tell me more about yourself?

ANDREW:

Modesty is important to me. I don't like to boast or appear to
boast. Anyway, my life's been very ordinary, not much to tell.
JACQUI:

I suppose. I've had a few friendships that have turned to
relationships.

ANDREW:

Mmm?

JACQUI:

Still, you can never get enough. Friends, that is.

ANDREW:

No.

JACQUI:

(looks at watch)

Oh, I'd better go. I didn't realise it is so late. You must come to mine.

ANDREW:

Yes, I will. Let me walk you home.

JACQUI:

That's kind, but no. I can handle myself. Bye.

ANDREW:

Mmm.

Scene 6: LOC: CITY CENTRE: DAY

(JACQUI is shopping, getting her scarf at Ryder and Amies, looking in the market etc. She then wanders back to Agnes College and goes to the Porter's Lodge...

Scene 7: LOC: PORTER'S LODGE: DAY

PORTER:
Miss! Jacqui!!

JACQUI:
Yes.

PORTER:
There's a letter for you. Here.

JACQUI:
Thanks. It must be from my parents, about them coming up for a few days. Can you book them a guest room?

PORTER:
Of course, just let me know in advance.

JACQUI:
Thanks, I'll tell you this evening, when I get back from my date.

PORTER:
Oh yes. Already dating, are you?
(smiles knowingly)

Scene 8: LOC: UNIVERSITY CENTRE DINING ROOM: NIGHT

(ANDREW and JACQUI are both dressed up for the evening. They are facing each other across the table)

ANDREW:

You look lovely tonight.

JACQUI:

Thanks. So do you.   I love the light from these, it's very romantic.

ANDREW:

I know. I love it here. It's even better with you here.

JACQUI:

(smiles)

ANDREW:

I don't come out with the best chat up lines. Sorry.

JACQUI:

It's nice.   (smiles) Your parents local?

ANDREW:

L.A.

JACQUI:

L.A. America? Wow, mine are in Hampstead.

ANDREW:

Very nice. Nice area. Yeah, they live over there mostly but they have a property over here too.

JACQUI:

They'll be up next weekend. I'd love you to meet them, and maybe come out with us.

ANDREW:

I'd love to.

JACQUI:

That's a date then?

Scene 9: INT: WILLIAM'S BEDROOM: NIGHT

(WILLIAM and HELEN are in bed)

HELEN:

Here's your Ovaltine, dear.

15

WILLIAM:

Ah, thank you. I love having our Ovaltine together. Routine in an ever changing world.

HELEN:

Yes dear. Look, I'm having lunch with an old friend tomorrow. Can you manage to do yourself lunch?

WILLIAM:

Oh yes, I'll go to the grad pad. Should show my face there once in a while.

HELEN:

Good idea.

WILLIAM:

Do I know her? This old flame.

HELEN:

No.

WILLIAM:

Everything is alright isn't it dear?

HELEN:

What? Ur, yes, of course. Why shouldn't it be?

WILLIAM:

I don't know. You just seemed a bit…preoccupied today.

HELEN:

Just thinking what to talk about with my old flame.

WILLIAM:

Oh. I see. That's alright then. I do love you, old girl.

HELEN:

Me too. (kisses him) Goodnight.

Scene 10: LOC: PUB: NIGHT

(HELEN and MR CALLAN) are at a corner table, drinking and chatting.

HELEN:
It's nice to see you again.

MR CALLAN:
Yes.

17

HELEN:

Not staying long, then?

MR CALLAN:

No, just visiting my son. He's at Agnes. He's been telling me about this lovely girl, he's met.

HELEN:

Oh that's nice. My husband is having his new students round one by one. Had a very pretty girl the other day. Jacqui, I think her name was.

MR CALLAN:

Really? My Andrew's girlfriend is called Jacqui.

HELEN:

Well it's a small world.

MR CALLAN:

William doesn't know about us, does he?

HELEN:

No. He doesn't think I have it in me to be unfaithful so thoughts like that don't occur to him. Besides, I think he has his mind on certain other people himself at the moment.

MR CALLAN:

Who?

HELEN:

Jacqui. You know, things haven't been easy lately. There's tension between us. He'd never admit it and I mean there's nothing outward, it's just...the sex isn't...well it just doesn't happen any more.

MR CALLAN:

I think the world of you, Helen, you know that.

HELEN:

I know. I love my William and I wouldn't want to hurt him but I just feel my life's going nowhere. It's the same routine. I stay at home and tend the garden and do the housework, and cook dinner. William bathes, then I bathe, then we have two mugs of Ovaltine or Horlicks while we sit up in bed and listen to Radio 4, and then we kiss each other good night and go to sleep. We don't even move. If it wasn't for the dents in our pillows one would never know we'd been in it.

MR CALLAN:

I'm sorry to hear that. And I'm sorry I can't be here more often. It's just my work keeps in Milton Keynes so much.

Long hours, you know. But the salary's so good I can't say no.

HELEN:
I'd better get going. If I'm out too long, William starts getting suspicious. But why I don't know. I told him I was having lunch with an old flame, and he just assumed it was a woman. Maybe he doesn't see me as feminine enough that other men could want me. Maybe I'm just like a soppy old dog that fetches his slippers. (snivels)

MR CALLAN:
I'm sure he knows you're beautiful. Maybe he's got some problem he can't bring himself to admit to. Have you thought of that?

HELEN:
No.

MR CALLAN:
Why don't you talk to him?

HELEN:
Alright, but I still want to see you again.

MR CALLAN:

Of course. Come on, let me drive you home.

HELEN:

Thank you.

Scene 11: INT: JACQUI'S ROOM: DAY

(JACQUI hugs her parents as they arrive)

JACQUI:

Thanks for coming up so soon.

MRS HILLMAN:

Well, we miss you already, and we so love Cambridge.

(pause) How are you getting on?

JACQUI:

Really well. But I've missed you and I do think about home.

Anyway, I thought we could do some shopping tomorrow. In

the evening, I've asked Andrew to join us. It will give you a

chance to meet him.

MRS HILLMAN:

Ah, the new man.

MR HILLMAN:

Got the important things sorted, haven't you Jaqs!

JACQUI:

Of course.   (smiles) You know me.

Scene 12: INT: ANDREW'S ROOM: DAY

(ANDREW is with his parents)

ANDREW:

You should have told me you were coming. I'd have booked
you a room.

MR CALLAN:

No, no. We're happy at The University Arms. We wanted to
surprise you.

ANDREW:

It's a very nice surprise.

MRS CALLAN:

It was a bit impromptu actually.

ANDREW:

Yes.

MRS CALLAN:

Your father had to see his LAMDA teacher.

ANDREW:

Oh yes, how's that going?

MR CALLAN:

Very well thanks. I haven't seen her for a while. Not until this weekend anyway.

MRS CALLAN:

And in Aisha's absence, you're staying faithful I hope?

ANDREW:

Of course.

MR CALLAN:

This girl, Jacqui.

ANDREW:

What about her? How do you know about her anyway?

MR CALLAN:

A little bird told me.

ANDREW:

Oh, yes. I forgot you moonlighted as a scarecrow.

MR CALLAN:

Very good. Just you don't forget Aisha, that's all. I know she's a long way away but she's a nice girl and I don't want her getting hurt. Female company is fine, but there's a line, and you mustn't cross it.

Scene 13: INT: JACQUI'S ROOM: NIGHT

(ANDREW and JACQUI kiss)

MRS HILLMAN:

Well, it's nice to finally meet you Andrew.

MR HILLMAN:

Jacqui hasn't stopped talking about you.

ANDREW:

All good I hope.

MRS HILLMAN:

Oh yes, you're quite a catch.

ANDREW:

Thank you. I can see where Jacqui gets her looks from.

MRS HILLMAN:

Flatterer!

JACQUI:

We've booked some guest seats at formal halls for you both.
You'll love it.

Scene 14: LOC: CLARE BRIDGE: MOONLIGHT

MR CALLAN:

I hope Andrew's not playing around. He looked very
sheepish if you asked me and it won't be the first time.

MRS CALLAN:

Don't worry.

MR CALLAN:

I mean, who doesn't take his parents out for the evening
when they come.

MRS CALLAN:

We did arrive unannounced. He's probably had existing
arrangements.

MR CALLAN:

Alright.

MRS CALLAN:

It's very hard for him, with Aisha in L.A. He must have some
female company.

MR CALLAN:

Well, he knows the score. I've told him he's to keep it in his
trousers, or words to that effect.

MRS CALLAN:

Indeed.

Scene 15: LOC: KING'S PARADE: MOONLIGHT

ANDREW:

I don't have a girlfriend as such. Jacqui coming over to me
that night was fate.

MR HILLMAN:

Well, you seem to have your future all mapped out. Our
Jacqui wants to go into Forensics.

ANDREW:

Yes, she said.

MRS HILLMAN:

Your parents are here this weekend too I gather. I hope this
date wasn't awkward.

ANDREW:

Not at all. I wasn't expecting them. They'll be alright.

JACQUI:

I have to see my supervisor tomorrow but you'll be alright
shopping and things won't you.

MRS HILLMAN:

Yes. Maybe we can meet up in the evening.

JACQUI:

Yes.

Scene 16: INT: WILLIAM'S LOUNGE: DAY

(JACQUI is sitting close…)

WILLIAM:

It seems Andrew's every bit the English gentleman, despite being American.

JACQUI:

I know, but it just seems too perfect. He's been here three years and hasn't been snapped up.

WILLIAM:

Why don't you mention it, subtly mind. If he loves you, he'll tell you the truth. I'm sure of it.

JACQUI:

I don't know. It might look like I don't trust him or something.

WILLIAM:

You don't though.

JACQUI:

Oh, I don't know. I don't want not to trust him, but as I said, it just seems so unlikely that he'd be unattached after so long.

WILLIAM:

There really is only one way to find out.

JACQUI:

I know.

WILLIAM:

Bite the bullet and ask. Feel the fear and do it anyway. There's a psychological mantra for you!

Scene 17: LOC: COFFEE BAR IN MARKET: DAY

(JACQUI and ANDREW are at the table with coffees...)

JACQUI:

Andrew, is there something you're not telling me? I get the feeling your parents may not approve of us.

ANDREW:

I didn't want to have to tell you this, but I'd better. It isn't that I have a girl. I just have a few things on my mind.

JACQUI:

What things?

ANDREW:

My parents want me to return to L.A. when I finish my doctorate.

JACQUI:

They can't make you, Andrew!

ANDREW:

Oh, they can, Jacqui. Believe me.

JACQUI:

How?

ANDREW:

I have a big inheritance waiting for me. And a w…

JACQUI:

A what?

ANDREW:

A wonderful future. My father knows a lot of people. He could get me into Harvard no problem, imagine that.

JACQUI:

What about us?

ANDREW:

You could come to America.

JACQUI:

No, I couldn't. I'm too much of a home girl.

ANDREW:

Well, I've got a while to go yet. Why don't we just muddle along and cross each bridge as we come to it.

JACQUI:

Okay. I suppose that will do.

Scene 18: INT: WILLIAM'S LOUNGE: EVENING

JACQUI:

Sorry to be here again, and unannounced.

WILLIAM:

Don't worry. I'm always happy to see you. Don't worry about Andrew. He'll probably stay on after his PhD. Americans love to boast about their children's' achievements, especially a doctorate from Cambridge. Anyway, you shouldn't put all your eggs in a basket. Go out in the evening. Go pubbing and clubbing. The men will be falling over themselves. There's an S.U. dance tonight. Take my advice. Go back to your room, tart yourself up, and go out and have a bloody good time. William's orders!

JACQUI:

Alright, I will.

WILLIAM:

(smiles)

Scene 19: INT: STUDENT UNION HALL/BAR: NIGHT

(There is a frenzy of activity, loud music etc. JACQUI is sitting by the bar, looking around and inviting approaches. TRISTAN approaches...)

TRISTAN:
Hi.

JACQUI:
Hi.

TRISTAN:
Drink?

JACQUI:
Thanks, gin and tonic please.

TRISTAN:
Lager top and G & T please.

BARMAN:
Coming up.

TRISTAN:
What are you doing on your own, looking so gorgeous?

JACQUI:

What's the next chat up line, by the way, I'm a doctor?

TRISTAN:

How about, I'm a medical student? It's true.

JACQUI:

Are you?

TRISTAN:

Yeah. Two years to go.

JACQUI:

I'm doing Psychology at Agnes.

TRISTAN:

Oh right. I'm at King's.

BARMAN:

£2.30 mate.

TRISTAN:

(hands him a fiver) Have one yourself.

BARMAN:

Cheers.

JACQUI:

(takes her drink and sips it)

TRISTAN:

How about a dance?

JACQUI:

Well, actually, I could use some fresh air.

(They step outside)

TRISTAN:

Both my parents are medical. Dad's a surgeon, and mum's a
midwife. Dad always hoped I'd follow in his footsteps.

JACQUI:

My dad's a civil servant. Mum works in M & S. I hope to do
Forensics.

TRISTAN:

How glamorous.

JACQUI:

Fancy coming back to my room?

TRISTAN:

Yeah, great.

Scene 20: INT: JACQUI'S ROOM: NIGHT

(Gentle ballads are playing on the radio)

JACQUI:

It's only a single. Still, that's an advantage.

TRISTAN:

It certainly is.

JACQUI:

I'm glad I went to the dance. My supervisor said I should, and it paid off.

TRISTAN:

Who's your supervisor?

JACQUI:

William Hunter-Bletchingley.

TRISTAN:
Yes, I had him for some of our abnormal psychology
modules.

JACQUI:
Now, that's spooky.

TRISTAN:
Yes.

JACQUI:
(kneels on the bed) Come on, Tristan.

TRISTAN:
(kneels opposite)

JACQUI:
You can take my bra off if you like.
(SHE bends forwards)

TRISTAN:
You're really something, aren't you Jacqui.

(Lap dissolve)

Later...

(JACQUI and TRISTAN are lying on the bed alongside each other)

JACQUI:
That was wonderful, Tris.

TRISTAN:
It was.

JACQUI:
Do you want to know what I like about you?

TRISTAN:
Yes.

JACQUI:
Your sensitivity. For a rugby player, you're quite gentle really.

TRISTAN:
I'm playing next week. Why don't you come and watch?

JACQUI:
Okay.

TRISTAN:
Are you seeing anyone else?

JACQUI:

Um, no. Well, nothing serious.

TRISTAN:

Okay. I just wondered if you wanted to be exclusive?

JACQUI:

Already?

TRISTAN:

Yes, sorry. I'm rushing things. It's all gone to my head.

JACQUI:

Your blood hasn't.

TRISTAN:

(gentle laugh) You were so fantastic.

JACQUI:

Thanks.

TRISTAN:

You're right. Let's keep things steady and see what happens.

Scene 21: LOC/INT: PUB: DAY

(ANDREW and PAUL are at the bar when JACQUI enters)

ANDREW:
So what do you think of her then Paul?

PAUL:
Gorgeous.

JACQUI:
Hi Andrew. You must be Paul.

PAUL:
And you *must* be Jacqui.

JACQUI:
Yes. Nice to meet you. I hear you swing both ways.

PAUL:
What?

JACQUI:
(gasps) Oh sorry. I don't know why I said that.

PAUL:

(laughs) It's alright. Yes, yes I do.

JACQUI:

Is it better that way?

PAUL:

It's like being able to enjoy VHS *and* DVD.

JACQUI:

Right.

ANDREW:

(To JACQUI) You were out last night when I called.

JACQUI:

Oh yes, I forgot to tell you. I went to the Student Union dance.

ANDREW:

Was it good?

JACQUI:

Oh, the sex was great. I mean, the dance was great. Yes, sorry, I was…

ANDREW:

Yes, well, as long as you enjoyed yourself. Meet anyone?

JACQUI:

Sort of.

ANDREW:

Uh huh?

JACQUI:

Can one of you get me a coke?

PAUL:

Sure.

ANDREW:

(beckons Jacqui close) Jacqui. Am I your first lover?

JACQUI:

No. Not that it's any of your business.

ANDREW:

Do you want me to make love to you?

JACQUI:

Come again.

ANDREW:

Do you want me to make love to you?

JACQUI:

That's what I thought you said. (pause) I'll get back to you
on that.

PAUL:

Here's your coke, Jacqui.

JACQUI:

Thanks Paul. Cheers!

Scene 22: INT: WILLIAM'S BEDROOM: NIGHT

WILLIAM:

So it's tomorrow that you leave for London?

HELEN:

Yes, but it's only for a few days.

WILLIAM:

I know, but I worry dear. Neither of us is as young anymore.

HELEN:

Don't worry. Just drink your Ovaltine.

Scene 23: INT: ANDREW'S ROOM: MORNING

(ANDREW's alarm clock sounds. He is bleary eyed. His clothes are strewn everywhere and JACQUI is asleep beside him. They are in their underwear...)

ANDREW:

(stirs)   Oh hell, my parents are due this morning? I need a coffee. (nudges JACQUI) Wake up Jaqs.

JACQUI:

(opens eyes blearily) Mmm. Oh, morning Tristan.

ANDREW:

Morning who?

JACQUI:

Oh, sorry, Andrew. (pause) What are you doing in my bed?

ANDREW:

You're in my bed.

JACQUI:

What?! Shit!! It's nine thirty. Your parents will be here in a minute, and you stink of drink!

ANDREW:

We all got on to heavier stuff as time wore on. They hate drunkenness.

JACQUI:

Alright, stay calm. I'll chuck the bottles out of the window and you have a shower with some of that pine gel of yours. I'll open the windows and spray air freshener around. Now get up! Go on!

(the doorbell rings)

ANDREW:

Shit!!

JACQUI:

Just get in the shower!

ANDREW:

Yes, miss.

JACQUI:

I'll go out the back window. You count yourself lucky I don't mind climbing down a drainpipe half naked.

(she exits)

ANDREW:

See you later then.

(the doorbell rings again, and it is ignored by ANDREW who goes for a shower)

Scene 24: LOC: CITY CENTRE (MARKET): DAY

(JACQUI and TRISTAN are walking past the C.U.P, shop when they see ANDREW with his parents. She pulls TRISTAN close and turns her back...)

TRISTAN:

What's up?

JACQUI:

I just...hang on. Just don't look for a minute, okay?

TRISTAN:

What's the matter?

JACQUI:

(peers round) It's okay, you can look now.

TRISTAN:

Thanks. But what was that all about?

JACQUI:

Nothing. Come on, let's go.

(They pass the coffee/tea stall. HELEN and MR CALLAN are there...)

HELEN:

My husband's unlikely to come by today.

MR CALLAN:

It's lovely to see you again so soon. Thank you for agreeing to come to London with me.

HELEN:

I'll enjoy it. It'll be nice to see your new place.

MR CALLAN:

I want my wife to be surprised when I tell her I passed. I don't want her to think I'm having an affair or anything.

HELEN:

I understand completely. It's the same with my husband. Oh, your family is coming over.

MRS CALLAN:

Hello, dear. I don't think we've been introduced.

HELEN:

I'm an old friend. Helen.

MRS CALLAN:

Well, well. Small world.

ANDREW:

Hello. You're William's wife aren't you?

HELEN:

Um, yes. Yes.

ANDREW:

How do you two know each other then?

HELEN:

We met once. Well, a few times.

MRS CALLAN:

Well, drink up dear. We have to get back to the hotel.

MR CALLAN:

Well, no, I'm going to the flat in London today, remember.

MRS CALLAN:

Oh yes. Well, shouldn't you be getting going.

MR CALLAN:

The Cambridge Cruiser at 11.15 will get us there for midday.

It's right near King's Cross and I'll be back this evening.

MRS CALLAN:

Alright. Well, Andrew and I will amuse ourselves. Come on Andrew. See you later dear.

MR CALLAN:

Mind you, it is ten thirty and we had better get going. We'll get a cab. (pause) Cambridge seems to be going downhill. My son smelled of drink when he found us in the market and when we rang this morning, there was no answer. He said some drunken students had poured some beer over him last night. Dreadful isn't it?

HELEN:

Well, you always get the odd lout. That's the way of the world. There's a fair youth population round Cambridge that is native you know. Not all the young people here are students.

Scene 25: INT: JACQUI'S ROOM: NIGHT

(JACQUI and TRISTAN flop onto the bed…)

JACQUI:
Whoo! It's good to have a rest. Nice idea, taking in a film.

TRISTAN:
Yes. Who were you staring at in the front row?

JACQUI:
I thought I saw Andrew's parents.

TRISTAN:
Andrew?

JACQUI:
Oh, I'd better tell you. Before I met you I made friends with his post-grad Arts student, Andrew. He wanted to get serious but he's going to L.A. when he finishes his Master's degree so there's no future for us. His parents were here to see him. Strange he wasn't with them.

TRISTAN:
Was he the reason you had your funny few minutes in the market the other day?

JACQUI:

Yes.

TRISTAN:

And you've slept with him?

JACQUI:

I think so. I don't really know. We were a bit drunk.

TRISTAN:

Oh God, listen to me. I'm sounding all possessive. I'm sorry.

JACQUI:

That's okay.

TRISTAN:

If he keeps bothering you, I'll sort him out.

JACQUI:

I know. Come on, let's go to bed.

(JACQUI turns out the light)

Scene 26: LOC: PORTER'S LODGE: NIGHT

(AISHA arrives with her suitcases…)

AISHA:
Excuse me.

PORTER:
Yes miss.

AISHA:
Hi, I'm looking for Andrew Callan.

PORTER:
Oh, sorry miss, he doesn't live in college rooms. His place is over the other side of Clare Bridge on the ring road. If you wait a minute I'll give you the address.
(HE goes off to find it, then returns)   123 Queens Road.
Shall I call you a cab?

AISHA:
Yes please.

PORTER:
I'll do that for you now, miss.

AISHA:

Thanks.

Scene 27: LOC: OUTSIDE ANDREW'S FLATS: NIGHT

(The taxi pulls up and the driver gets her luggage out, then leaves. AISHA drags the cases up to the porch and rings but there is no answer. A while later, ANDREW arrives…)

ANDREW:

(shocked) Er…Aisha?!!

Scene 28: INT: ANDREW'S LOUNGE: DAY

(AISHA and ANDREW are having a light breakfast)

AISHA:

Did you miss me poppet?

ANDREW:

Of course.

AISHA:

Another year at John's Hopkins and I'm finished. I hope.

(the doorbell rings)

ANDREW:

I'd better go.

AISHA:

No, leave it. We have to talk.

(It rings again. JACQUI is seen outside looking up, she then leaves)

ANDREW:

What is there to talk about?

AISHA:

Well, I haven't seen you in ages, so, a lot. Second, we have to sort out what's happening when I finish at John's Hopkins. Am I coming over here? Do I wait for you to finish and you come back to L.A? You know your mom wants you to.

ANDREW:

Yeah, and dad. I don't know. I've been here so long, it's kind of....this is my home now. Well, it feels like home. Yeah, it's cold and wet and quaint but I like it.

AISHA:

No, hon. Everyone looks like a fox hunter and smells like a Labrador.

ANDREW:

It's not that bad. The students are a hip crowd even if the academics and their families are a bit stuffy.

AISHA:

Yeah, well. We need to talk.

ANDREW:

Okay. Why don't we have some tea in the garden?

AISHA:

Gee, you are English aren't you?

ANDREW:

I can do coffee.

AISHA:

No, no. Tea's fine. When in Rome and all that.

ANDREW:

Yeah.

AISHA:

And then we'll go into town.

ANDREW:

Whatever you want.

Scene 29: INT: JACQUI'S ROOM: DAY

TRISTAN:

So why did you go to Andrew's this morning then?

JACQUI:

I don't know. Just to talk I guess. He didn't answer.

TRISTAN:

Maybe he was out early.

JACQUI:

No, as I walked away I saw the curtains move. And at
lunchtime I saw him with this gorgeous woman in the market.

TRISTAN:

So what, I thought you were only friends.

JACQUI:

I was just…curious.

TRISTAN:

Forget about him. We've got each other now.

(There is a knock at the door. JACQUI answers)

ANDREW:

Jacqui!

TRISTAN:

Jacqui?

JACQUI:

Oh, Andrew.

TRISTAN:

I'd better…

JACQUI:

No, no. You stay.

TRISTAN:

Thanks, I will.

ANDREW:

Tristan Campbell. Kings, right?

TRISTAN:

Yes. You were something big in the Student Union weren't you?

ANDREW:

Vice President.

TRISTAN:

Well, well. Still here then. How's Aisha?

JACQUI:

Who?

ANDREW:

Er...Aisha. Oh, she's fine.

TRISTAN:

Up at the moment is she?

ANDREW:

No.

TRISTAN:

Oh, right. It's just I swear I saw you two in the market at lunchtime.

ANDREW:

Oh, well, yes, she's up. I mean, she's here. For a few days that's all. Just to say hello.

JACQUI:

Was she the beautiful woman I saw you with in the market at lunchtime?

ANDREW:

I'm surprised Tristan hadn't told you.

JACQUI:

No. She an old girlfriend is she?

ANDREW:

Well, not girlfriend exactly. Look, I'd better go. See you.

JACQUI:

I think it's time I paid Aisha a visit.

Scene 30: LOC: OUTSIDE ANDREW'S FLAT: MAIN DOOR: DAY

JACQUI:

(rings bell. After a minute, AISHA answers)
Hello.

AISHA:

Yes?

JACQUI:

I've come to see Andrew. I'm Jacqui.

AISHA:

Oh, right. I'm Aisha. I'm his fiancée.

JACQUI:

F...f....fiancee?

AISHA:

Yeah, come in. I'd like to talk to you for a while.

JACQUI:

Okay.

(the door closes)

Scene 31: INT: ANDREW'S LOUNGE: DAY

AISHA:

So, where do you fit in then?

JACQUI:

Well, I'm his…sort of girlfriend. Well, I thought I was.

AISHA:

What, as in, sex together girlfriend!

JACQUI:

Sort of.

AISHA:

You can't sort of have sex. Either you have or you haven't!

JACQUI:

He asked me. I said I'd think about it. Then we got drunk
and I can't remember whether we did it or not. Honest.

AISHA:

Well Andrew sure wasn't.

(SHE hears the door)

AISHA:

Here he is. My God, he's going to wish he hadn't come back.

ANDREW:

(enters) Hello, I...(gasps) Oh shit!

JACQUI:

I've just been getting to know your FIANCEE!!!!

ANDREW:

I can explain.

AISHA:

Well, we're waiting.

ANDREW:

Look, Jacqui. Aisha was in L.A. I hadn't been with a woman for years. I just wanted some local company.

JACQUI:

Local company! Oh right. So it's not because you love me...

ANDREW:

No, I do.

JACQUI:

But because you can't shag Aisha because she's in the States! She's your fiancée for God's sake. When were you planning on telling me? I asked you weeks ago if there was someone else, and you said there wasn't.

ANDREW:

Well you don't tell a girl you're seeing about your fiancée do you? Unless you're a complete dickhead.

AISHA:

You're scum. All this time I've been loyal to you while you've been thousands of miles away!

ANDREW:

Can't prove it though, can you?

AISHA:

Are you calling *me* a liar? That's rich, coming from you.

JACQUI:

We know you're a liar, Andrew. How many other girls have you charmed, shagged and dumped in a single term? How many hearts have you broken?

ANDREW:

Don't exaggerate.

AISHA:

If this wasn't your flat, I'd kick you out you son of a bitch! I'm going back to L.A. tomorrow to hang out, sleep around and get some sort of a life back!!

(SHE storms out)

ANDREW:

Jacqui?

JACQUI:

Get away from me!

(SHE leaves too)

ANDREW:

Jacqui!!

Scene 32: INT: WILLIAM'S LOUNGE: NIGHT

JACQUI:

I know it's late but I needed to talk to someone.

WILLIAM:

I never mind you dropping in, you know that. Don't worry too
much. You do need to keep things in proportion. You've got
Tristan now. The two of you are happy together – what's the
problem? It doesn't matter what Andrew does or who he
sees does it?

JACQUI:

No, but…what with him lying and then having a fiancee
without telling me. I feel used

WILLIAM:

We've all been there my dear. I had the same problem with a
girl. I thought she loved me. It turned out she'd slept with

most of Cambridge. Broke my heart when I found out. But who knows? I might never have met Helen if that hadn't happened. You see, every cloud has a silver lining. Life events happen for a reason, Jacqui. I really do believe that.

JACQUI:
Well, yes, I believe in destiny too. I think fate brought Tristan and I together.

WILLIAM:
There we are then. I mean, it's not like you slept with Andrew is it?

JACQUI:
I did. I think.

WILLIAM:
And have you told Tristan?

JACQUI:
Sort of.

WILLIAM:
Sort of honest then?

JACQUI:

I guess so. But it isn't the same. I wasn't engaged to someone else when I did it. What he did was far worse. And now Aisha's left him and I feel guilty about that.

WILLIAM:

It's Andrew's fault, not yours.

JACQUI:

Guess so.

WILLIAM:

Talk to Tristan. He'll understand. He seemed a decent sort of chap as I recall from the odd time I lectured to him.

JACQUI:

I hope so.

WILLIAM:

Trust me. Will you talk to him?

JACQUI:

Okay. Thanks William. I'd better get to bed now.

WILLIAM:

See you soon.

Scene 33: INT: JACQUI'S ROOM: DAY

(The telephone rings...TRISTAN answers...)

TRISTAN:
Hello?

ANDREW:
Who's that?

TRISTAN:
Tristan, remember.

ANDREW:
Oh yes, can I talk to Jacqui a minute?

TRISTAN:
No, she doesn't want to speak to you. And I don't blame her!
(puts phone down)

JACQUI:
(on bed) Thanks, Tris

Scene 34: INT: WILLIAM'S BEDROOM: NIGHT

WILLIAM:

(sipping his Ovaltine) Helen, tell me. Who are you really seeing when you go on these weekends and business meetings?

HELEN:

Alright. I can't blame you for being suspicious but its nothing really. He's a pupil of mine I'm coaching for his ALAM exams.

WILLIAM:

I thought you'd stopped that. You know it was affecting your health.

HELEN:

It's only him. I had to prove I could still do it. Do you see?

WILLIAM:

Of course. And I'm very proud of you.

HELEN:

Mr Callan, his name is.

WILLIAM:

Not...Andrew Callan's father?

HELEN:

Jacqui's Andrew? Oh, as was. Maybe. He said he was visiting his son.

WILLIAM:

Well well, how fortuitous. You can keep me posted!

HELEN:

Well, he's back in London now, for a while. I'm going to see him again soon. But I'm not having an affair with him. That'd be like you having one with Jacqui.

WILLIAM:

I'm not having one with Jacqui! (coughs quietly) Oh, sorry. (smiles)

Scene 35: LOC: FIREWORKS: NIGHT

(Amongst the crowd by a roaring bonfire…)

JACQUI:

This is just what I need. A good fireworks show.

TRISTAN:

I love them. And it's such a nice fresh evening too.

WILLIAM:

(taps JACQUI on the shoulder)

Hello again.

JACQUI:

(startles)

Oh, hello William. Helen. This is Tristan.

TRISTAN:

Hello.

WILLIAM:

Nice to see you.

JACQUI:

Andrew hasn't been in touch since…you know.

WILLIAM:

Probably best.

HELEN:

So, Tristan. You're the man that's won our Jacqui's heart.

TRISTAN:

Yes. And I consider myself very lucky.

WILLIAM:

I'm off to the clubhouse for a real ale. We'll see you later.

HELEN:

I'm going over there dear, less crowded.

WILLIAM:

Won't be long.

(THEY go their separate ways)

JACQUI:

What a lovely couple.

TRISTAN:

Mmmm. We will be too.

JACQUI:

I hope so.

ANDREW:

(comes towards them)

JACQUI:

Speak of the Devil.

TRISTAN:

(To ANDREW) What do you want?

ANDREW:

Hello to you too.

TRISTAN:

Don't get funny with me.

JACQUI:

Tris, it's okay. (To ANDREW) We'll talk some other time,

okay. Not now.

ANDREW:

Jacqui!!

JACQUI:

Go away!

ANDREW:

(turns and walks away)

TRISTAN:

That's my girl.

WILLIAM:

I've just had a thought, why don't you join me for an ale?

JACQUI:

Not really my thing.

WILLIAM:

Oh, I suppose it wouldn't be, no.

TRISTAN:

I won't say no. Look, I'll buy. You can have something light darling.

JACQUI:

Okay.

WILLIAM:

I'll have a Eagle Blackeye then Tristan.

TRISTAN:

Okay, I'll get them in. See you there.

JACQUI:

No, we'll miss the fireworks. Bring them back.

TRISTAN:

Okay. I'll get a tray.

JACQUI:

He's so wonderful, my Tris.

WILLIAM:

Good.

JACQUI:

You alright, William?

WILLIAM:

Yes, yes. Just thinking, letting my thoughts wander, you know.

JACQUI:

Yes.

WILLIAM:

I really am happy to see you anytime. To help you. I'd do it for all my students.

JACQUI:

Would you? Really?

WILLIAM:

Well, alright. I have a soft spot for you. You're so full of life. My Helen…well, I've said enough. I mustn't burden you with my problems.

JACQUI:

Problem? Helen?

WILLIAM:

We don't…not for a long time, you know.

JACQUI:

Right.

WILLIAM:

I just feel awkward about mentioning it, and now…I think she's having an affair.

JACQUI:

I'm sure she isn't. She wouldn't.

WILLIAM:

I hope you're right. I can't lose her. I love the old girl to bits. I wouldn't try anything with you. I'm old enough to be your granddad.

JACQUI:

Good. I think you're a kind and wise man, but nothing romantic.

WILLIAM:

Okay, good. What should I do about Helen?

JACQUI:

Well, talk to her. Has she got the wrong idea about how you feel for me perhaps?

WILLIAM:

I hadn't really wanted to think about that. I suppose she might have done, as she saw me lingering over your essay.

JACQUI:

Oh.

WILLIAM:

Oh indeed.

TRISTAN:

Here are your drinks.

WILLIAM:

Thanks Tristan. Cheers. Cheers Jacqui.

JACQUI:

Cheers. Here's to everything working out well for all of us.

WILLIAM:

I'll drink to that. Now I must go and locate Helen.

(Fade)

Scene 36: LOC: WINTERY CAMBRIDGE STATION: EXT

Caption: CHRISTMAS

(TRISTAN's train is about to leave)

TRISTAN:
I'll miss you Jacqui.

JACQUI:
I'll miss you too. But we won't be apart for long.

TRISTAN:
I'll ring you, and I'll see you Boxing Day.

JACQUI:
We're all really looking forward to that.

(TRISTAN boards his train, and as it leaves, he waves
goodbye. JACQUI is left alone on the platform, waving back)
(Fade)

Scene 37: INT: JACQUI'S FAMILY HOME: LOUNGE: DAY

(JACQUI, TRISTAN and Jacqui's parents are sitting round the fire)

JACQUI:
I had a lovely Christmas.

TRISTAN:
Me too. Although this last fortnight seems to have been terribly long without you.

JACQUI:
Tristan and I can still go to the New Year's Eve do on the South Bank can't we.

MR HILLMAN:
Of course. I'm sure you'll have a great time. You've had a hard term, and you both deserve a treat.

TRISTAN:
Well, thank you for putting up with me for a week.

MRS HILLMAN:
Our pleasure.

TRISTAN:

We're going to my folks after New Year.

MR HILLMAN:

Yes, Jacqui told us. Where do they live?

TRISTAN:

Torquay.

MR HILLMAN:

Oh lovely. Lovely part of the world, the West Country.

TRISTAN:

Well, I must say, Highgate's pretty classy isn't it.

MRS HILLMAN:

Not bad is it? We've been here, oh…what…about ten years
now, haven't we dear.

MR HILLMAN:

Yes, we used to live in Shepperton, by the film studios. You
could see the sets from our back garden.

TRISTAN:

Pretty close, then.

MRS HILLMAN:

(smiles)

JACQUI:

Tristan's going to follow his parents into medicine.

MRS HILLMAN:

Yes, that's right. I always think if you can keep something in the family, it's a wonderful thing.

MR HILLMAN:

I wouldn't wish the Civil Service on Jacqui, that's for sure.

Scene 38: INT: JACQUI'S BEDROOM: NIGHT

(THEY are sitting by the window)

TRISTAN:

Aren't the stars lovely tonight.

JACQUI:

It's very romantic, just the two of us. In the starlight.

TRISTAN:

A taste of married life.

Scene 39: LOC: NEW YEAR'S PARTY: NIGHT

Caption: New Year's Eve

(The noise of the party is going on. JACQUI and TRISTAN are on the terrace. It's nearly midnight)

TRISTAN:

(holds JACQUI's hands)

Jacqui, there's something I must say. You're very special to me. I want us to be together always. When we finish our studies, I want us to spend the rest of our lives together. So I wondered…(takes small box out of pocket)…Would you do me the honour of becoming my wife?

JACQUI:

(opens box, stunned) It's beautiful. Of course I will.

TRISTAN:

(hugs her)

JACQUI:

(reciprocates)

(Big Ben's chimes ring out and fireworks and cheers ring out)

Scene 40: LOC: SENATE HOUSE: CAMBRIDGE: DAY

Caption: The New Term

JACQUI:

I just can't get over how happy I feel being engaged to you.

TRISTAN:

Our parents were delighted too. My father's paying for the wedding.

JACQUI:

Mine are paying for the honeymoon.

TRISTAN:

It couldn't be more perfect.

JACQUI:

Even if your clinical placement is far away, I'll wait for you.

TRISTAN:

I know. Come on, let's see where I'm going.

(They look at the notice board outside the Senate House)

TRISTAN:

(gulps) Guys!

JACQUI:

That's great, Guys!

TRISTAN:

It's the best placement. I'll be away from you though. Seven weeks.

JACQUI:

No, stay at my parents' place. They won't mind, and I can see you at weekends. It's not far from Guy's.

TRISTAN:

I couldn't impose.

JACQUI:

Shall we ask?

TRISTAN:

Guess so. The worst they can do is say no.

(As they leave, ANDREW comes and looks at the placements...)

Scene 41: INT: WILLIAM'S LOUNGE: DAY

JACQUI:

So, it's all worked out really well.

WILLIAM:

Great. You two will be very happy I'm sure, and our congratulations again. But keep one foot on the ground though. It's the mock lab practical this term. It's still important even though it's only a mock.

JACQUI:

Okay.

WILLIAM:

Do you have a hypothesis?

JACQUI:

Yes, whether or not, and how quickly blind mice develop compensatory senses.

WILLIAM:

Very good, but we don't have any blind mice, do we?

JACQUI:

No, I've thought of that. I've developed a mouse blindfold.

WILLIAM:

(chuckles) What a refreshing change to have a scientist with a heart! Good luck to you.

Scene 42: LOC: MARKET: DAY

(JACQUI is pondering over a coffee, when ANDREW approaches and sits...)

ANDREW:
Jacqui, please talk to me.

JACQUI:
Can't you take a hint?

ANDREW:
Just let me explain.

JACQUI:
I don't want to hear it.

ANDREW:

Well, you're going to.

JACQUI:

You lied to me from the start, cheated on me…

ANDREW:

Look, I just thought with Tristan away at Guy's that you'd…

JACQUI:

What?! How did you know he was at Guy's?

ANDREW:

Um…it's common knowledge isn't it?

JACQUI:

No.

ANDREW:

Ah.

JACQUI:

You looked on the boards at the Senate House didn't you?
You're pathetic Andrew.

ANDREW:

Jacqui.

JACQUI:

Get lost! I don't want to see you again, understand?

(HE leaves, slowly)

(PAUL comes over)

PAUL:

Hi. Can I join you?

JACQUI:

Paul, sure.

PAUL:

Andrew's been very depressed lately. Do you know if anything's happened?

JACQUI:

No, I'm sorry. It's just...well he's engaged to a girl in L.A., has been for years. He was while he was seeing me, and now I've met her. He lied to me, Paul. Lies, lies, lies.

PAUL:

Oh God. I'm sorry. He never told me Aisha was his fiancée.

JACQUI:

Well, it looks like we've both been taken for a ride then, doesn't it.

PAUL:

Yep.

JACQUI:

I don't care anymore, Paul. I really don't.

Scene 43: LOC: OUTSIDE ANDREW'S FLAT: EVENING

(TRISTAN and JACQUI are walking by when they see an ambulance outside and a body being wheeled out on a stretcher)

JACQUI:

Andrew!!

TRISTAN:

(grabs her arm) Jacqui, getting yourself run over won't help.

JACQUI:

Oh God!

TRISTAN:

Calm down, calm down. Come on, let's see what's going on.

JACQUI:

(to ambulance man) Is that Andrew? Can I see?

AMBULANCE MAN:

And you are?

JACQUI:

I'm his ex-girlfriend.

AMBULANCE MAN:

(shrugs) Alright.

JACQUI:

(lifts blanket and screams) It is!!

TRISTAN:

Oh no.

JACQUI:

(hugs TRISTAN) It's Andrew!

TRISTAN:

Alright, alright. Come on, have a hug.

JACQUI:

Oh God, he's killed himself. It's all my fault.

TRISTAN:

No. It's not.

JACQUI:

It is. I didn't have to see Aisha. I should have stayed out of it.

TRISTAN:

You'd have found out eventually. It's not your fault, Jacqui. Listen to me. It is not your fault! He cheated on you. He deserved what he got. Come on, he's responsible for his own life, not you.

JACQUI:

I know you're trying your best, but there's only one person I can see right now. Sorry, Tris. I'll catch you later.

TRISTAN:

No, you shouldn't be alone.

JACQUI:

Alright. But I have to see William.

TRISTAN:

I'll get a cab and take you there. I can always wait outside.

JACQUI:

I don't deserve you.

Scene 44: INT: WILLIAM'S LOUNGE: NIGHT

WILLIAM:

I know. Mr Callan's been crying down the phone to Helen for
the last half hour. Overdose apparently. Drink and drugs you
know.

JACQUI:

It's so terrible William, and I'm to blame.

WILLIAM:

No, you're not. Come on Jacqui, it's only because you knew him, and you've got a lot of stress at the moment, with the lab tests pending. You'll be fine.

JACQUI:

I have to face his parents at the funeral. They'll know what I did.

WILLIAM:

They were as disgusted as you were when Aisha told them. Mr Callan's told Helen all about it. If it's any consolation, he feels just as bad. He told Andrew off about it only a few weeks ago, just after Christmas. Went on about how he was a disgrace, and he never wanted to see him again. Now he never will. Imagine how *he* feels. He won't bear you any malice. Anyway, you could always not go.

JACQUI:
True.

WILLIAM:

But between ourselves, because I shouldn't tell you this before the results come out, John Hamilton marked your paper and was very impressed. He knows about Tristan too.

Apparently his name cropped up once or twice, obviously in error. (HE chuckles)

JACQUI:
(faint smile) Obviously. Thanks, William.

WILLIAM:
Helen and I will be at the funeral. You won't be alone.

JACQUI:
Tristan and Paul are coming too.

WILLIAM:
Good.

(Fade…)

Scene 45: LOC: FUNERAL BY GRAVESIDE: DAY

(The camera moves in slowly as the vicar is heard conducting the service, and JACQUI and everyone are standing round...)

VICAR:

So, we commit the body of our dear brother, Andrew, to the earth. (coffin is lowered) May he rest in peace. Amen.

GENERAL:

(murmur) Amen.

JACQUI:

(turns away)

MR CALLAN:

Jacqui.

JACQUI:

Oh excuse...

MR CALLAN:

No, stay please. I know we never met you in person, but 'til now but please, don't feel guilty over Andrew's death. It was a lot of things...us, the MPhil, Aisha leaving him... It would have come to a head eventually.

JACQUI:

Do you truly forgive me?

MRS CALLAN:

Of course dear. We both do. He was always a bit wayward.

MR CALLAN:

There's nothing to forgive. I saw him after our argument before Christmas and patched things up. He knew we loved him and were proud of him even though what he did was wrong. Everyone makes mistakes. We're both hurting right now, but we don't want you hurting too. Please join us at the small gathering we're about to host.

JACQUI:

Alright, thanks. I'd love to.

(Fade)

Scene 46: INT: WILLIAM'S BEDROOM: NIGHT

HELEN:

End of term reports dear?

WILLIAM:

Progress reports before the end of year exams.

HELEN:

You seem to be lingering over that one.

WILLIAM:

It's Jacqui's.

HELEN:

That explains it then.

WILLIAM:

You know, despite having had so much upheaval this year, she had a good lab prac result, and her essays have been fine. I wouldn't be at all surprised if she got a 2:1 this summer.

HELEN:

Look, William dear, I know there's something else on your mind. Apart from Jacqui. We must talk.

WILLIAM:

Alright. You first.

HELEN:

Are you having an affair with Jacqui?

WILLIAM:

Heavens! No! I told Jacqui too. She thought I was for heaven's sake. I said she was very beautiful but I was too old for her and I loved you too much to ever be unfaithful. I'm sorry things have got so mundane. I'm sorry old girl but I just don't have the energy I used to. But if you...um, how can I put this...need a visit from Roger...then you shall have one.

HELEN:

Oh darling! That's been on my mind so much, the fact we never have sex. The fact you don't think I need it because I'm so loyal to you. That's why you thought my old flame was a woman, you just assumed!

WILLIAM:

No, I thought because you always tell me so much about your life you'd have mentioned it if you'd had a gentleman friend.

HELEN:

Why?

WILLIAM:

I don't know.

HELEN:

Anyway, the *gentleman friend* is my soul LAMDA student. He's Andrew's dad, he loves his wife and I love you. I admit I thought about it for the sex but I'd never have done it.

WILLIAM:

Come on, let's make things right.

HELEN:

Oh, you're just an old romantic at heart aren't you?

WILLIAM:

Yes.

Scene 47: LOC: THE BACKS: DAY

TRISTAN:

The months seem to be going so fast. Nearly exam time.

JACQUI:

I know. All my coursework's been great so far, but I'm worried about the exams. I know we're having a wonderful time together, but I still find myself thinking of Andrew. I so wish I'd never looked at his body.

TRISTAN:
I know. We all do things that with hindsight we wish we hadn't done. One moment really can change everything. Have you seen his parents since the funeral?

JACQUI:
No.

TRISTAN:
Good that William and Helen are happy again.

JACQUI:
Yeah.

TRISTAN:
Everything will be fine Jacqui.

JACQUI:
I know. I know. (kisses him)

(Fade...)

Scene 48: LOC: THE CORN EXCHANGE: DAY

Caption: Exam period

TRISTAN:

It may sound like a contradiction in terms, but you can hear the silence can't you.

JACQUI:

It's obviously exam time.

TRISTAN:

Good luck darling, you'll do brilliantly.

(Fade)

(Later...)

JACQUI:

That went pretty well.

TRISTAN:

Great.

JACQUI:

Have you been waiting here for me all the time?

TRISTAN:

I haven't moved. I could only think of you.

JACQUI:

Oh, that's so sweet.

TRISTAN:

I've got mine tomorrow.

JACQUI:

Well, I'll be here, waiting for you.

TRISTAN:

Lovely, that thought will help me get through.

(Fade)

Scene 49: INT: WILLIAM'S LOUNGE: DAY

WILLIAM:

So, the exam fortnight's finally over, and the year.

JACQUI:

Yes, and all things considered, I feel quietly confident.

WILLIAM:

Good. Well, you're a bright girl, so I'm sure you'll be fine. I predicted you a good degree on my progress report.

JACQUI:

Tomorrow, Tris and I are off the the Senate House for the results.

WILLIAM:

Fingers crossed then.

Scene 50: LOC: SENATE HOUSE: DAY

(THEY are looking at the exam results boards…)

JACQUI:
(squeals) Yes! Yes!!

TRISTAN:
I haven't heard that for a while!

JACQUI:
I got a 2:1. Tris, I got a 2:1!!!

TRISTAN:
Well done!!

JACQUI:
Thank you. And you?

TRISTAN:
Yes. Me too!! I'm onto my pure clinical years now!

(THEY hug each other, WILLIAM comes over)

JACQUI:
William?

WILLIAM:

I had to be here to share your joy. I knew what you'd got last night in truth. And Helen? Her student passed his ALAM exam, Mr Callan that is, despite his son's death.

JACQUI:

She was coaching him?!

WILLIAM:

Yes. Her last...ever...student.

JACQUI:

Well give them my congratulations.

WILLIAM:

And we send you ours. Well done both of you! I'd better go now. I have to see John Hamilton for lunch.

JACQUI:

Wasn't that sweet of him to come all the way over.

TRISTAN:

Says it all really, doesn't it.

JACQUI:

He's a genuinely nice man. A father figure. He *has* been this year, that's for sure.

TRISTAN:

And now we've got the whole summer together.

(FADE)

Scene 51: STUDIO/LOC: SENATE HOUSE INTERIOR. DAY

Caption:
Two Years Later – Graduation Day

(TRISTAN's parents and JACQUI's parents join the other parents and friends along the sides of the Senate House. It is dimly lit. The Vice Chancellor sits on a throne like chair on the raised platform at the end, dressed in scarlet and white fur robes, ready to hold the hands of each student as they are admitted to the University…)

JUNIOR PROCTOR:

Agnes College.

(TRISTAN, JACQUI and some other graduates step forward)

PRAELECTOR:

Dignissime domine Domine Procancellarie et tota Academica,
praesento vobis hos viros et has mulieres quos scio tam
moribus quam doctrina esse idoneos ad gradum
assequendum Baccalaurei in Artibus; idique tibi fide mea
praesto totique Academiae.

JUNIOR PROCTOR:

Stephanie Anne Fraser...

(She steps forwards, kneels at the Vice Chancellor's feet and
offers her hands, which he holds and they look into each
other's eyes...

VICE CHANCELLOR:

Te etiam admitto ad eundem gradum.

(SHE takes one step back, bows and walks out through the
door behind the VC)

JUNIOR PROCTOR:

Jacqui Gina Anne Hillman.

JACQUI:

(comes forward)

VICE CHANCELLOR:

Te etiam admitto ad eundem gradum.

JACQUI:

(bows and leaves)

JUNIOR PROCTOR:

Hannah Jane London....

(LAP DISSOLVE)

PRAELECTOR:

Dignissime domine Domine procancellarie et tota Academica,

praesento vobis hos viros et has mulieres quos scio tam

moribus quam doctrina esse idoneos ad gradum

assequendum Baccaleurei in Medicina; idique tibi ide mea

praesto totique Academiae.

JUNIOR PROCTOR:

Tristan Alistair Campbell.

TRISTAN:

(steps forward)

VICE CHANCELLOR:

Te etiam admitto ad eundem gradum.

(CUT TO)

Scene 52: LOC: OUTSIDE THE SENATE HOUSE: DAY

(Groups of graduates are standing on the lawsn being
photographed, others are milling with their families and
friends, the camera rises over the rails to witness a parade of
graduates coming down Trinity Street towards the Senate
House for their degree ceremony…JACQUI and TRISTAN
are with their parents, WILLIAM and HELEN)

WILLIAM:

You must be so proud of them. And with the wedding next week too, it really is so wonderful isn't it.

MRS HILLMAN:

And I hear it's in no small part thanks to you William.

WILLIAM:

Just part of the service. (winks at JACQUI) Oh, excuse me. I need a quick word with the Praelector.

TRISTAN:

I've had the most wonderful three years with you.

JACQUI:

Me too. Now we've graduated, we're getting married – oh I'm so happy.

TRISTAN:

So am I. I love you so much.

JACQUI:

I love you too. This is the best day of my life! So far.

Scene 53: LOC: OUTSIDE COUNTRY CHURCH: DAY

(Confetti is showered as the happy couple walk out...bells ring out)

MRS HILLMAN:

(crying) Oh, how my little Jacqui's grown.

WILLIAM:

(puts his arm round her) I knew she'd come through. They make such a lovely couple don't they. I only have faint memories of my wedding day to Helen...it was a while ago now.

MRS HILLMAN:

(smiles)

(JACQUI and TRISTAN are shown into a white limousine, and the car drives away, as the crowds wave...)

Scene 54: LOC: INSIDE CAR: DAY

JACQUI:

I love you, Mr Campbell.

TRISTAN:

I love you two, *Mrs* Campbell.

THE END